How to get ready for Christmas:

Write a letter to Santa

Dear Santa,

Decorate yourself with baubles

Sing some nice Christmas songs

Wear fancy trousers to keep your bottom warm on Christmas Eve

For
Colin Williams and Michelle Forde

HODDER CHILDREN'S BOOKS
First published in Great Britain in 2016 by Hodder and Stoughton

1 3 5 7 9 10 8 6 4 2

Text and illustrations copyright © Alex T. Smith, 2016

The moral rights of the author have been asserted.

A CIP catalogue record for this book is available from the British Library.

ISBN: 9781 444 92649 1

Design by Alison Still
Printed and bound in China

The paper and board used in this book are made from wood from responsible sources.

FSC

Hodder Children's Books
An imprint of Hachette Children's Group
Part of Hodder and Stoughton
Carmelite House, 50 Victoria Embankment, London EC4Y 0DZ

An Hachette UK Company
www.hachette.co.uk

www.hachettechildrens.co.uk

SANTA CLAUDE

ALEX T. SMITH

Hodder
Children's
Books

In a rather festive house on
Waggy Avenue, there lives a dog.
A small, plump dog.

Claude

A jaunty
jumper

Sir Bobblysock

A small, plump dog called Claude,
who wears a jaunty jumper and a
very snazzy beret.

Claude lives with Mr and Mrs Shinyshoes and his best friend Sir Bobblysock, who is a very bobbly sock.

Whenever Mr and Mrs Shinyshoes are out of the house, Claude and Sir Bobblysock go on an adventure. What adventure will they have today?

'Twas the night before
Christmas and Mr and Mrs
Shinyshoes were off to a party
in the city. They were looking
terribly glamorous.

'See you later!' said Mrs
Shinyshoes, slipping into
her slingbacks.

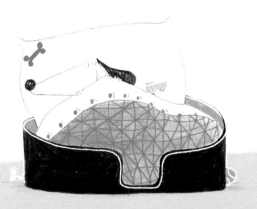

'We'll be back at midnight!'
cried Mr Shinyshoes,
straightening his dickie bow.

Then they both blew kisses
towards Claude, who was fast
asleep, and clattered out of the
front door into the snowy night.

Claude waited a few moments…
listening…

When he was absolutely sure
that he and Sir Bobblysock were
alone in the house, he pinged
open his eyes and sat up in bed.

Then he flung everything
out of his beret and had a
jolly good root around in it.

Gosh!
 He was
  ever so
    excited!

'AHA!' he cried eventually
(in his Outdoor Voice), and
from the depths of his hat he
produced an **enormous**
hardback book.

He'd been really looking
forward to reading it since
his friend and favourite police
person, PC Anne Cuffs, had
presented it to him with his
very own pair of special police
handcuffs to say thank you
for rescuing her earlier that
afternoon.

11

Claude and Sir Bobblysock
had discovered her dangling
from her utility belt, her legs
waggling and the keys on her
key ring jangling. She'd been
decorating the police station
when the ladder slipped and
left her hanging in midair.

Claude had quickly righted
the ladder and spent the day
helping Anne with the tree.
Sir Bobblysock thought he
looked lovely draped in
tinsel, but that's
another story…

13

PC Anne Cuffs wasn't the
only person Claude and
Sir Bobblysock
had helped
that week.

They'd fed the pigeons.

They'd helped Beverly
Clematis, the florist,
make holly wreaths
for people's knockers.

They'd sung some lovely Christmas songs with their friend Carol Singer's choir…

(Claude didn't really know the proper words so he just made them up.)

Deck the halls and jingle your bells!

Here comes the Christmas hippo! She's wearing a lovely hat!

And they'd been kept very busy
indeed at the post office! Percy
Package, the postman, had been in
a real tizz with all the letters for
Santa until Claude and Sir
Bobblysock had bustled in to help.

Percy helped the children stick
stamps on their letters.

Claude helped put their letters in great big sacks.

Sir Bobblysock helped by sitting on a swizzly office chair with a clipboard and made sure everyone did everything properly.

At the end of the day there was just time for Claude to write his own letter to Santa, which he did in his best handwriting. Then he stuck a stamp on it and popped it in the sack with the others. He wasn't sure what he really wanted for Christmas, so he asked for a surprise!

Dear Santa,
Please can I
have a surprise
for Christmas.

Claude x

Santa Claus
The North Pole

'I wonder what would happen
if I stuck a stamp on myself
and sat in one of these bags?'
thought Claude.

TO: THE
NORTH
POLE

Thankfully Percy spotted
Claude just as the bags were
being loaded into a big van to
be sent to the North Pole.

20

Back in his cosy bed on
Christmas Eve, Claude
snuggled down in the darkness
to read his new Cops and
Robbers book. Then he
rummaged around in his beret
once again and took out his
special reading lamp, and
switched it on.

21

It was a clever head torch – just
perfect for reading when you had
a big, heavy book and your paws
were really rather on the small
side. And it left your hands free
for dunking biscuits in a nice
cup of tea, which is never
a bad thing.

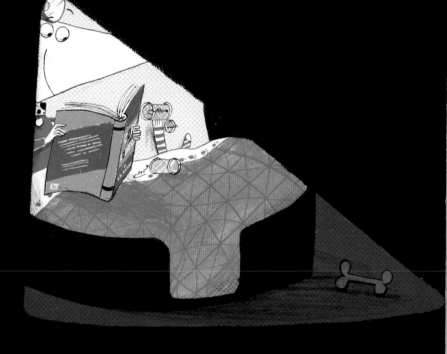

Sir Bobblysock busied himself
carefully jabbing hairpins into
his curlers to keep them nicely
in place and Claude settled
down to read his book.

Goodness!
It was exciting!

Claude flicked through the pages
to show Sir Bobblysock – there
were dastardly robbers, brave
police officers, thrilling car
chases and –

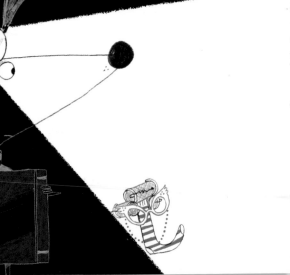

'I think someone is IN our house!' hissed Claude. His eyes grew big and wide like saucers and his bottom wiggled his tail about like billy-o – half with nerves and half with giddy excitement.

Sir Bobblysock was all a-quiver too. His specs were steamed up and his curlers were askew.

THUD!
THUD! THUD!
THUD!
THUD!

Whoever could it be? Who on earth could have snuck into their house on Christmas Eve?

Claude suddenly gasped! He knew exactly who it was…

A BURGLAR! A burglar! Right here on Waggy Avenue!

His eyebrows started to waggle with excitement. This was absolutely the start of an adventure and his big chance to catch a burglar RED-HANDED just like a police officer!

'Claude,
you are
a hero!'

Cor! he thought.
Wouldn't his friend
PC Anne Cuffs be
proud of him!

27

Claude fished around in his beret for his handcuffs, switched off his head torch and tiptoed ever so quietly to the door.

Sir Bobblysock really wanted to supervise from the safety and comfort of his bed, with his head under the covers, but thought he'd better help out.

'After three!' whispered Claude with his hand on the door.

CRASH!

Claude thundered into the pitch-black living room. He barged into the burglar's knees and pushed him to the ground. Then he clapped the handcuffs around his wrists and locked them –

CLINK!

– around the arm of a chair.

Sir Bobblysock then hoofed in
and bopped the intruder on the
nose with a rolled-up magazine
for good measure.

'HA HA!'

cried Claude
triumphantly. 'Now let's see
what you look like, you naughty
robber!'

And he switched on the lights.

Uh… oh…

It wasn't a burglar handcuffed
to the armchair…

It was…

'SANTA!?'

gasped Claude.

Claude wondered if someone had turned the radiators up because he suddenly felt a bit hot under the head torch. Sir Bobblysock had one of his tropical moments.

Claude fussed with the hem of his jumper and quickly explained to Santa how he thought he might actually have been a robber.

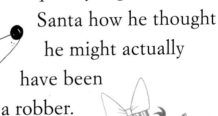

'I'm very sorry…' he said in a
quiet voice.

'Don't you worry!' said Santa,
chuckling. 'Now would you mind
awfully letting me out of these
cuffs? I've got a jolly
busy night tonight.
Have you got the
key handy?'

Claude blinked for a moment.
A key… Yes, there ought to be
a tiny key for those handcuffs,
but where was it?

Quickly Claude found his
beret and emptied the
contents out again onto the
carpet. Then he looked in all
the nooks and crannies.

36

Finally, he peered under his jumper and inside his shoes.

Sir Bobblysock went to check if the key was in the pocket of his quilted bed jacket or in his sewing box, but it wasn't.

In fact, it wasn't ANYWHERE!

'Oh dear! Oh dear!' sighed Santa.
'Whatever will we do? I have all
these presents to deliver before
the sun comes up…'

Claude ran his foot around in a
circle. This WAS a problem! And
he'd caused it… If only he could
help in some way…

Suddenly he had an idea!

'We can do it!'

he shouted. 'We have to be back by midnight, but I'm sure we'll get them all delivered by then!'

Santa wasn't very sure at all, but didn't really know what else he could do.

'It's jolly cold flying about in the sky on a sleigh,' he said. 'Do you have a coat?'

Claude nodded and wiggled into his toasty anorak.

'You might need something to keep your botty warm too...' said Santa. 'Why don't you borrow my lovely trousers?'

They were a **bit** big but Claude tucked his anorak into them and pulled the belt buckle tight.

'Finally,' said Santa, 'you'll
need this,' and he popped his
special hat on top of Claude's
beret. Claude looked very
smart. Sir Bobblysock
admired his
pompom.

'Now, to get up and down
the chimneys easily,' Santa
continued, 'you must remember
to tap the side of your nose.
Then you'll whizz up and down
no problem!'

Claude nodded.

Sir Bobblysock carefully wrapped
a headscarf over his curlers,
Claude tapped the side of his
nose, and just as Santa had said
the two friends whipped
magically up the chimney.

On the roof was a very handsome
reindeer and a beautiful sleigh.
On the back of it, in the biggest
bag Claude had ever seen, were
hundreds and hundreds and
HUNDREDS of presents.

It was going to be a jolly busy night.

Claude and Sir Bobblysock
hopped into the driver's seat
and with a flick of the reins
they were off. Whooooooooosh!
Up into the sky on their very
important
mission!

The first house was a bit tricky. Claude forgot
to do Santa's special nose-tapping trick,

so ended up hurling himself
down the chimney with
Sir Bobblysock rattling
along behind him.

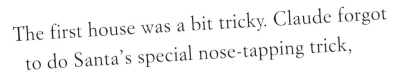

The two friends exploded into
the living room in a great big
cloud of soot and dust!

Claude quickly piled up the presents under the tree, put the cookies addressed to Santa Claus under his beret for later and skedaddled back up the chimney.

Sir Bobblysock hoped one of the presents was a vacuum cleaner to clean up all that mess.

48

In the next house, Claude got his foot caught up in a string of fairy lights on the way back up onto the roof.

In the third, he knocked over the
Christmas tree and in the fourth
he startled someone's pet parrot.

'SQUARK!'

went the parrot.

'GREAT GLITTERY BAUBLES!'
cried Claude in surprise.

'GREAT GLITTERY BAUBLES!'
shouted the parrot, who liked to
repeat things.

'Shh! You silly sausage!' hissed Claude.

'SHH, YOU SILLY SAUSAGE!'

yelled the parrot.

Sir Bobblysock said that that was the problem with parrots – there was no talking to them – so he and Claude whooshed back up the chimney leaving the parrot all alone shouting about sausages and baubles…

At the next house there was a
problem. It didn't have a chimney.

How on earth are we going to
get in? wondered Claude, as
he parked the reindeer in the
front garden.

The two friends checked the
doors and windows, but they
were all locked shut.
Then Sir
Bobblysock
spotted
something –

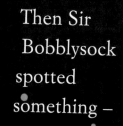

999
LETSBY
AVE.

It was a cat flap.

'Well done, Sir Bobblysock!'
hollered Claude. He smoothed
down his ears, sucked in his
tummy and squeezed through
the little hole with an armful
of presents.

Sir Bobblysock followed behind
very carefully so as to not upset
his curlers and
         headscarf.

The two friends put out the presents under the tree and Sir Bobblysock excelled himself at titivating all the bows and parcel tags.

'Super dooper!' said Claude. 'We're really getting the hang of this now!' He stepped back to admire their work and...

Over went a plate of biscuits
and a glass of milk –

SMASH!

– onto the floor!

Sir Bobblysock was just thinking
that the tissue he'd left tucked
up the arm of his cardigan at
home would be very useful just
now when from upstairs there
came a voice.

'Hello? Is someone
there?' it called, and
footsteps sounded
on the staircase.

'YIKES!'

yelped Claude. 'Quick! No one
is meant to see us!' And the two
pals ran for the cat flap.

Sir Bobblysock hopped out easily,
but when Claude dived through –
oh dear! – he forgot to suck in
his tummy and he got well and
truly WEDGED.

'Help, Sir Bobblysock!' he cried.
'Quickly, before I'm caught!'

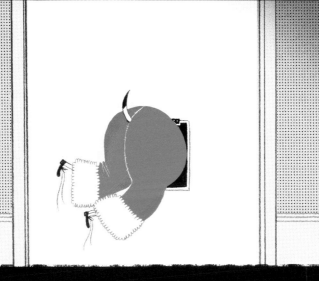

But it was too late!

Behind Claude there were
footsteps. Then the door he was
wedged in swung open and
standing in front of him was...

PC Anne Cuffs.
In her nightie.
With her hands on her hips.

'Claude! What on earth are
you doing dressed as Santa
Claus and stuck in my cat flap
in the middle of the night?'

She gently pushed Claude's
bottom through the cat flap
and he told her all about what
had happened.

He explained how he'd accidentally handcuffed Santa Claus to the armchair at home, how he'd lost the key and how he'd borrowed Santa's special warm trousers and hat so that he and Sir Bobblysock could go out to deliver presents.

'But,' he said finally, 'we've only delivered parcels to five houses and we need to get them all done before Mr and Mrs Shinyshoes come back home at midnight OR we need to think of a way to get Santa out of those handcuffs...'

He sighed and Sir Bobblysock
did too, partly to copy Claude,
but mainly because he wanted to
be in the warm again and could
hear his bed jacket calling.

sigh...

'Midnight?!' exclaimed Anne Cuffs. 'But, look! It's almost midnight now!' She showed them the time on her watch. Ten minutes to go!

'Oh no!'
cried Claude, panicking.
'WHAT
WILL
WE
DO?'

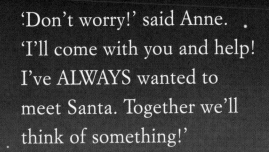

'Don't worry!' said Anne.
'I'll come with you and help!
I've ALWAYS wanted to
meet Santa. Together we'll
think of something!'

And so she and Claude
gambolled over the front of the
sleigh like the police did over
their cars in Claude's book. Sir
Bobblysock thought about doing
the same but his ankles were
stiff with cold and he was still
terrifically worried about his
curlers staying in place so he
gently climbed in and
settled himself under the
knee blanket.

WHIZZ!

Through the snowy air went the sleigh and a few minutes later, Claude, Anne and Sir Bobblysock crashed onto the roof of 112 Waggy Avenue and shimmied down the chimney with a tap of Claude's nose.

Santa was ever so glad to see them.

'I've tried everything to wiggle
my hands free,' he said, 'but they
won't budge!'

'Don't worry!' said Claude.
'We'll save you! Won't we?'

And he looked over at Anne
Cuffs, but she was so excited
to see Santa that she just stood
there with her mouth open.

Claude took her special
key ring to see if any of the
keys would unlock the
handcuffs.

But none of them did!

'The lock is too small!' he cried.

Claude rummaged around in his beret and brought out a saw. He could trying sawing through the handcuffs?

'No!' cried
Santa and Anne Cuffs.

The clock on the mantelpiece
struck midnight.

'Oh no! This is a disaster!'
said Claude, doing a funny little
panicky dance on the carpet.
'Mr and Mrs Shinyshoes will
be back any second!'

Indeed, at that very moment,
it sounded like a taxi was slowly
making its way down snowy
Waggy Avenue.

Sir Bobblysock was trembling all over with worry. His bobbles bobbled about, his specs were on sideways and his curlers jangled about under his headscarf.

'Sometimes, very naughty robbers pick the locks with something tiny…' said Anne Cuffs, 'like a hairpin or something…'

Claude's ears leapt up.

'A hairpin?!' he said. 'Would that work?' Anne nodded.

That was it!

Claude quickly jumped across the room and with one super-speedy swipe, he swept Sir Bobblysock up from the pouffe and jammed one of the hairpins holding his curlers in place into the lock.

Then he wiggled Sir Bobblysock.
And he waggled Sir Bobblysock.

'Quick!' said Claude. 'Do a jiggly little dance to help!'

But Sir Bobblysock felt shy and couldn't dance without any music so whilst Claude and Sir Bobblysock wobbled about, Santa and Anne Cuffs sang some hearty Christmas songs.

Outside, there were footsteps coming up the steps.

JANGLE!

'Oh yikes!' cried everyone, but just then the knocker on the front door started to jangle…

CLICK!

The handcuffs pinged
open and Santa Claus was
FREE!!
'HOORAY!'
everyone shouted.

But Mr and Mrs Shinyshoes
were in the hall!

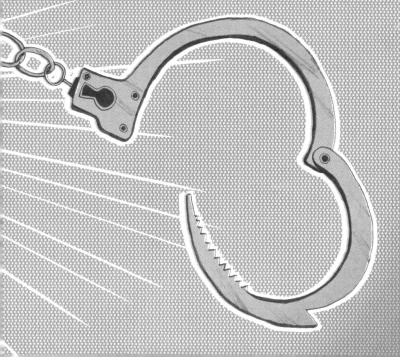

Claude gave Santa his hat and trousers back and he quickly bustled to the fireplace.

'Thank you!' cried Santa. 'Don't worry about all the other presents! Leave them to me!'

And he whooshed up the chimney.

'Good work, PC Claude!' said Anne Cuffs proudly. Then she saluted, hoiked up the living room window and hopped out into the night.

Claude and Sir Bobblysock
clicked off the light, leapt across
the room and dived into bed.

'Oh look...' whispered Mr
Shinyshoes, popping his head
around the door. 'Claude's been
fast asleep all night... What a
jolly good chap he is!'

When Claude woke up on Christmas morning, there were two neat little parcels addressed to him sitting on the floor beside his bed.

'Look, Santa Claus has left presents for Claude,' exclaimed Mr Shinyshoes.

Mrs Shinyshoes says 'I wonder what they are? Lets open them!'

One was a nice letter and stuck next to it was a teeny, tiny key.

WAGGY AVENUE POLICE DEPT
WAGGY AVENUE.

POLICE CHIEF: ANNE CUFFS

Dear Claude,

I found the missing
key - I'd mistaken it
for a decoration and
had accidentally hung
it on the police station
Christmas tree. Oops!
So sorry.

Love from A xxx

The second thing was a little box in which there was an ENORMOUS key ring and a little postcard with a lovely wintery scene of the North Pole on the front. On the back it said:

Thank you!
See you
next year!
Santa
xxx

NORTH POLE TOURISM LTD

POLAR POST

My friend Claude,
His bed,
The kitchen,
112 Waggy Avenue

'I wonder what they're all about?' said Mrs Shinyshoes. 'Do you think Claude knows anything about them?'

'Don't be silly!' laughed Mr Shinyshoes. 'Why would Claude need a tiny key and a gigantic key ring?'

But Claude DID know what he needed them for. And we do too, don't we?

Merry Christmas from Claude, Sir Bobblysock and all of your chums on Waggy Avenue!

Enjoy further Claude adventures:

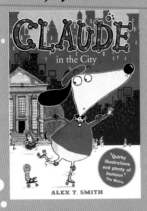

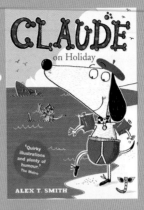

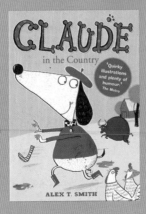

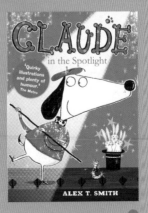

CLAUDE on the Slopes

'Quirky illustrations and plenty of humour.' The Metro

ALEX T. SMITH

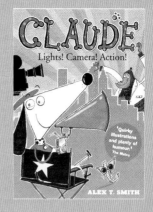

CLAUDE Lights! Camera! Action!

'Quirky illustrations and plenty of humour.' The Metro

ALEX T. SMITH

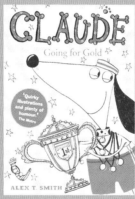

CLAUDE Going for Gold

'Quirky illustrations and plenty of humour.' The Metro

ALEX T. SMITH

SANTA CLAUDE

'Quirky illustrations and plenty of humour.' The Metro

ALEX T. SMITH

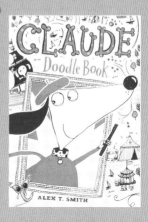

CLAUDE Doodle Book

ALEX T. SMITH

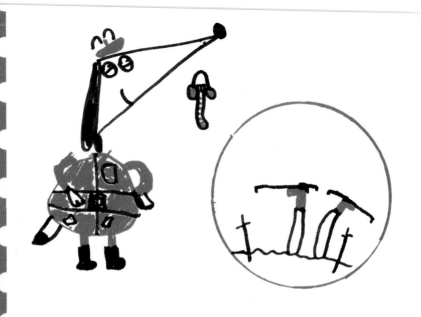

I like reading about Claude's super adventures as he always saves the day. Sir Bobblysock makes me laugh. He always stops for cake!

By Abigail, Age 6